DANCING FEET

TERESA HEAPY

Illustrated by
CATALINA ECHEVERRI

OXFORD
UNIVERSITY PRESS

OXFORD
UNIVERSITY PRESS

Great Clarendon Street, Oxford, OX2 6DP,
United Kingdom

Oxford University Press is a department of the University of Oxford.
It furthers the University's objective of excellence in research, scholarship,
and education by publishing worldwide. Oxford is a registered trade mark of
Oxford University Press in the UK and in certain other countries

First published in this edition 2019

British Library Cataloguing in Publication Data
Data available

978-0-19-276911-4

1 3 5 7 9 10 8 6 4 2

Paper used in the production of this book is a natural, recyclable product
made from wood grown in sustainable forests. The manufacturing process
conforms to the environmental regulations of the country of origin.

Printed in China

Helping your child to read

Before they start

- Talk about the back cover blurb. What mysterious thing might happen to Mabel when she watches a dancing show on TV?
- Look at the front cover. Think of two good words to describe the look on Mabel's face.

During reading

- Let your child read at their own pace, either silently or out loud.
- If necessary, help them to work out words they don't know by saying each sound out loud and then blending them to say the word, e.g. *p-l-i-nk-y, plinky.*
- Encourage your child to keep checking that the text makes sense and they understand what they are reading. Remind them to re-read to check the meaning if they're not sure.
- Give them lots of praise for good reading!

After reading

- Look at page 64 for some fun activities.

Chapter One

Mabel Green was doing Saturday morning ballet lessons.

Mabel Green *hated* Saturday morning ballet lessons.

She hated the prickly dress and the special shoes with elastic that bit into your feet.

She hated the plinky music.

She hated pretending to be flowers or fairies.

But most of all, she hated having to be *inside* dancing on a Saturday morning, when she could be *outside* playing football. Mabel was a defender for the Jesmond Juniors football team. They played matches every Saturday and Tuesday afternoon, and they practised on Saturday mornings. Mabel didn't like missing out on Saturday morning football practice in order to do *dancing*.

"*Why* do I have to do dance lessons?" she growled at Dad when he picked her up.

"Well, we just thought you might like to try it," Dad said brightly. "It's good for your coordination!"

Mabel Green was rather clumsy. Mabel Green knew this. She didn't like it to be mentioned.

She especially didn't like anyone to mention when she had slipped and missed that crucial goal.

Or when she'd fallen over and headed the ball into the Jesmond Juniors' own net.

And when a dive had turned into – well, a real dive, straight into a huge muddy puddle.

Her teammates were the same. The Jesmond Juniors team had broken the record for most matches lost (and the most mud splattered). Unsurprisingly, they were currently at the bottom of the junior league.

"I *hate* dancing," said Mabel. She took off her shoes and stuffed them in the bag. "No one *wins* anything. We just skip around tapping and pointing our toes. It's point*less* if you ask me!"

"Let's just give it to the end of term," said Dad. "OK, petal?"

Mabel gave her dad a withering glance.

That night, Mabel's friend Dora came over for tea. Dora *loved* dancing.

"Can we watch my favourite dance show?" she asked Mabel's mum. "It's called *Come Dance with Me*! I've got to see whether my favourite, Ted Turner, stays in the competition! Please?"

"Do we have to?" said Mabel. She'd had enough of dancing for today.

"Oh, come on, Mabel," said Mum. "We've never watched it, have we? Let's give it a try. I may even make some popcorn."

Mabel shrugged. "Oh well, if Dora likes it …"

Dora gave her a hug. "Thanks, Mabel! You'll love it!"

The Green family and Dora settled in front of the TV.

"And now …" said a deep, fruity voice.

"It's starting!" squealed Dora.

"*Live* from our TV studios, we proudly present … *Come Dance with Me*!"

Chapter Two

Sequins filled the screen, followed by the show's name, spelled out in large glittery letters.

"Oh no …" mumbled Mabel. She could already see this was not her thing *at all.*

A man wearing a shiny suit and a big white smile leaped on to the stage. "Welcome to *Come Dance with Me*!" he declared. The studio audience went wild. "Have we got a show for you!"

"It's Simon Shimmer!" whispered Dora. "He's the host! He's amazing! He can tap-dance *up the wall*!"

It got worse from there.

The show had celebrity dancers who all had to pick a member of the audience and then dance with them around the glittering floor.

Then it was time for the audience to vote, to keep the celebrities in the show.

"Come on, Mabel!" squeaked Dora. "We've got to vote for Ted Turner! He *needs* us!"

Ted Turner used to be in a boy band and had a funny little beard.

"You make the call, Mabel," said Mum. "Here's the number."

Mabel dialled the number. She sighed. This was such a waste of time.

"Hello?" said a grand-sounding voice at the other end.

"Hello. It's Mabel Green here and I'm voting for … what's his name again?" said Mabel.

“Mabel Green!” said the grand voice. “What a charming name!”

Mabel rolled her eyes.

Suddenly, Dora looked as if she’d swallowed all her popcorn at once. “Looook!” she spluttered, pointing at the TV.

“Shhh!” said Mabel. “Can’t you see I’m on the phone?”

Dora flapped frantically at the screen. “Yes – and you’re … you’re talking to *him*!” she gasped.

Mabel looked at the TV, where Simon Shimmer was smiling a wide, bright smile at her. "And do you like dancing, Mabel Green?" he said.

"M-me?" stammered Mabel. "You're talking to *me*?"

"Why, of course, Mabel Green!" smiled Simon Shimmer. "You're our Special Caller!"

Mr Green clutched Mrs Green in delight. Dora jumped up and down.

"Right, well, I just want … er … what was the question again?" asked Mabel.

"Do you like dancing, Mabel Green?" repeated Simon Shimmer. "Easy question, I know. I mean, who doesn't?"
He laughed heartily.

"Er …" said Mabel. She looked at her mum, dad and Dora. They all frantically nodded their heads at her and mouthed "Say *yes*!"

"Well …"

She turned back to the TV screen.

"If I'm honest …" Mabel continued.

She noticed a huge, golden glitter ball twinkling above Simon Shimmer's head.

"… Dancing isn't really my *favourite* thing," she said.

The glitter ball seemed to be shining brighter than ever on the TV screen. It dazzled Mabel's eyes. She blinked – once, twice, three times.

"I'd rather be playing football," Mabel said, staggering backwards, blinded by the sparkling light.

And then something strange happened. Mabel Green's feet began to tap.

Chapter Three

Mabel looked down at her feet. They still looked completely normal, in her fluffy, blue slippers.

But they were tap-tap-tapping away. And she hadn't told them to do anything of the sort.

"Hang on a minute," she said.

"Cool, Mabel!" said Dora. "I didn't know you were doing tap-dancing lessons!"

"She's not!" said Mabel's dad.

"Well, I'm sorry to hear you're not keen on dancing, Mabel Green," said Simon Shimmer, down the phone and on the TV. "But maybe you can show us some of your football moves next week … when you and a Lucky Friend join us on *Come Dance with Me*!"

"*What?*" said Mabel's mum and dad at the same time.

"Yes! It always happens!" said Dora, looking like she might burst with excitement. "The Special Caller gets to go on *Come Dance with Me*! Oooh, Mabel, can I be your Lucky Friend?"

"Bye, Mr Shimmer," said Mabel, trying to put down the phone while tapping across the living room. "Excuse me! Can we stop talking about *Come Dance with Me*? Has anyone else noticed there's something *wrong with my feet*?"

Mabel's mum, dad and Dora looked at Mabel's feet.

Her toes were still tap-tapping away.

They carried Mabel around the room in a swinging tap-dance routine.

Mabel tapped on the coffee table, swung around the lamp and ended a flourish on her knees. Mabel's face, however, did not match the routine. It was mightily puzzled – in fact, it looked horrified.

"What is going on?" Mabel said, as she tapped her way back up to standing again. "I'm not a *dancer*, I'm a *footballer*! Has this ever happened when you've watched the show, Dora?"

"Never!" said Dora.

"Mabel, this is amazing!" said her mum. "Jim, we need to enrol her in tap lessons right now!"

"I'm not doing any more dancing lessons!" yelled Mabel. Her feet took her off to the kitchen, where she grabbed a mop and started doing a new routine. She twirled the mop in time to a cheery tune which no one could hear.

Dora joined her and gleefully tried to join in. "It's the power of *Come Dance with Me*!" she said. "It gets everyone dancing!"

"Well, it's not getting me!" said Mabel firmly. Her feet, however, seemed to have other ideas. They swung her up in the air, and clicked their heels. Then they tapped her all the way around the kitchen and back into the living room, where she did an enormous leap on to the sofa, and landed with a waggle of her hands.

"What is going on?" wailed Mabel.

Chapter Four

From that moment on, Mabel Green's feet didn't stop dancing.

Her feet had managed to – just about – quieten down when she went to sleep. She woke up in bed to find that her feet were on the floor, toes gently tapping, as if they couldn't wait to get going.

"When's this going to wear off?" Mabel sighed, eating cornflakes while click-clacking around the kitchen table.

"Jim, I think we should tell her dance teacher!" said her mum.

"I wonder if we should tell the doctor," replied her dad.

After breakfast, Mabel's feet did change a little. They stopped tap-dancing.

They started to do ballroom dancing instead.

She waltzed as she cleaned out the gerbils.

She jived during Sunday dinner.

She did the tango on a walk in the park and did the salsa while doing her homework.

"You really should have a sit-down," said Dad.

"I'll try," said Mabel. She sat down, with her feet doing the quickstep under the table. "It's a bit tricky."

"Aren't you tired, dear?" said Mum.

"I'm fine," said Mabel. "But I think I'd like to go to bed now."

Mabel's feet did not stop dancing the next day at school.

She did the rumba down the road and pirouetted in the playground. She did the lindy hop in literacy and the samba during science.

"Mabel Green!" said Miss Castle, her teacher. "Will you please sit still!"

"I can't, Miss Castle, I'm sorry!" said Mabel. "My mum's given me a note."

Dear Miss Castle,
Mabel can't seem to stop dancing.
Sorry about that.
Best wishes,
Mrs Green

"Hey, Mabel, what's going on?" said Douglas, the Jesmond Juniors' striker. "Are you doing some form of new training?"

"Er, yes," said Mabel, "that's it – it's for my …" (what had Dad said?) "er … coordination! Of course," she added, "it's a real pain."

But secretly, Mabel Green was beginning to enjoy her non-stop dancing.

She had always been the clumsy one who fell over. Now, she was the one who made people ‘ooh’ and ‘aah’ with her amazing moves. She liked seeing their faces when she slid dramatically into a room. And she loved the applause at the end of each dance.

Mabel Green was beginning to wonder if she was meant to be a footballer after all. Maybe she was really (sssh, whisper it) meant to be a dancer instead.

Chapter Five

The next day, a reporter came to the school. Mabel was now doing every kind of dancing, from Bollywood to ballet.

"Are you the girl who can't stop dancing?" the reporter asked.

"That's me!" said Mabel, doing a complicated hip-hop routine.

"When did it start? How long's it been going on? What's your favourite dance?" said the reporter.

Mabel answered all the questions while twirling on her head. Then she posed for a photo in mid-air.

"And will you be performing anywhere?" said the reporter, busily scribbling.

"Er … I don't know," said Mabel.

"Yes – you'll see her on TV on Saturday in *Come Dance with Me*!" said Dora, proudly.

"Cor, Mabel, you are talented," said Dora, after they'd said goodbye to the reporter. "You've only been dancing for two days and you're already miles better than me."

"Hey, I've been doing ballet lessons for two months!" said Mabel.

"Yeeees … but that didn't really count, somehow, did it, Mabel?" said Dora.

"Er … no. You're right," admitted Mabel. "And now, I'm off to football practice – come on!" She took Dora's hands and whisked her off in a whirling polka dance.

The Jesmond Juniors team stared as the girls twirled their way on to the pitch.

“You are going to stop dancing, now, aren’t you, Mabel?” said Douglas.

“Hmm, there’s just a teeny problem there,” replied Mabel, trying – and failing – to hide a smile. “I can’t!”

“Well, you’d better try,” said Douglas, “because in case you hadn’t realized, we’ve got a match against Thugsford Juniors.”

“What?” said Mabel, her smile disappearing. She’d forgotten they were playing against Thugsford: the biggest, meanest team in the junior league.

They were lined up by their minibus. They didn't look very friendly.

Mabel's clumsy feeling came back to her, all of a sudden. She was going to end up making a fool of herself, like she always did. It didn't seem likely that football and dancing were going to mix.

"Ha!" said the biggest of the Thugsford team. "This'll be easy, guys. Look, they've got a *girl* on their team – and she's *dancing*!"

"Just you wait!" shouted Dora, as she ran off the pitch. "Mabel's going to run rings around you lot!"

And to everyone's surprise – including her own – Mabel did just that.

She twisted and turned so much in defence that the Thugsford strikers got dizzy. Then she did the quickstep up the field –

"You're meant to be in defence!" yelled the team coach

– and wiggled her way around until she was right in front of the goal.

"Shoot, Mabel!" yelled Dora.

Mabel paused, panting. This couldn't be happening to her. She was going to fall on her face, like she always did in football ...

"Come on, Mabel!" shouted Douglas. "You can do it!"

Mabel took a deep breath, and let her feet take over.

She flicked the ball on to her right foot – then on to her left – then on to her head.

Surrounded by defenders, Mabel swirled around until the ball fell off her head, landed back on her right foot – and, with a vigorous kick, flew straight into the goal.

Jesmond Juniors won 12–nil.

Mabel led the team in a country and western line dance to celebrate.

Chapter Six

The school held a special dancing assembly the next day to celebrate Jesmond Juniors' spectacular win. Everyone was dancing, even the teachers.

Mabel's interview was published in the paper.

A TV crew came along to film an interview with Mabel and Dora. Suddenly, they were celebrities, just like the dancers on the show.

"Wow, Mabel," said Dora, as they danced their way home. "This is brilliant. You're going to be amazing on *Come Dance with Me* on Saturday. And I can't believe I'm going to come with you!"

"Well, if you hadn't come over for tea and made me watch that programme," said Mabel, "none of this would have happened."

Saturday finally made its grand entrance, and Mr and Mrs Green took Mabel and Dora to the filming of *Come Dance with Me*.

Reporters were there to greet them as they came into the studios. Cameras flashed in their eyes as question after question was fired.

"Mabel Green, I think you might just be a tiny bit famous at the moment," whispered her mum. "So make sure you behave yourself and don't wipe your nose on your sleeve like you always do."

Mabel smiled, but inside she felt a quiver of worry. A school football match was one thing, but this was live TV. What if she fell on her face? What if something went wrong?

"You'll be great, Mabel!" said her dad. "Just trust your feet!"

Suddenly, the TV lights all went on at once, flooding the stage with light. Cameras zoomed in on the dance floor, scanning the audience.

"Welcome to … *Come Dance with Me*!" boomed a big voice, and Simon Shimmer appeared at the top of a long flight of stairs, which had lights set into every step. The audience went wild. He danced his way down the staircase, pausing every now and then to beam at the audience.

"Hello!" he called. "What a warm welcome – what a crowd you are! And I think we have an extra-special guest tonight …"

An enormous spotlight lit up Mabel.

"It's … Miss Mabel Green!" announced Simon Shimmer. "The girl with dancing feet!"

Chapter Seven

"I don't believe it!" squeaked Dora.

"Nor do I!" said Mabel. To her delight, her feet whisked her off her chair and on to the floor. She did a short routine, which took in ballet, tap and flamenco, finishing with a cartwheel.

"Yes, this is the girl who last week said she didn't like dancing!" beamed Simon Shimmer. "That's the power of *Come Dance with Me*, ladies and gentlemen! Look forward to seeing you later, Mabel!"

Mabel sat down to huge applause. She felt all warm inside now. She'd just done a cartwheel on live TV. She hadn't fallen over. She felt as if she could do *anything*.

The show was a great success. Dora, to her ear-piercing delight, was selected to dance with Ted Turner, who whisked her around the floor in a waltz. Each of the remaining four celebrities danced, and one, with tears of anguish, was voted out. A sea of dancers in top hats and feathers swept around the floor.

Then it was time for the finale.

Simon Shimmer appeared alone in the centre of the stage in his gleaming white suit. "And now, it's time for our final dance!" he smiled. "Mabel Green – will you *Come Dance with Me*?"

Stagehands moved the set into position – a huge glittery goal.

"Hey, they remembered you said you liked football!" said Mabel's dad. "Go on, petal – you show them what you can do now!"

Mabel made her way up to the dance floor, her feet sliding in rhythm to the music. A camera followed her as she sashayed towards Simon Shimmer's outstretched hand and his beaming smile.

Mabel looked up at him, happily – but, all at once, she found the golden glitter ball was directly behind his head. Suddenly, she couldn't see anything except a huge beam of light as the glitter ball twisted and twinkled in the glare of the cameras.

"Hold on …" she said. "I … can't see …"

"OK, Mabel," said Simon Shimmer. "It's your big moment!"

Mabel spun around, trying to see Simon Shimmer, but she could only see golden light from the glitter ball. She lurched backwards, blinded once again by the flickering gleam. She blinked in the light: once, twice, three times.

And suddenly, her feet didn't feel so sure of themselves.

and all at once, Mabel found herself falling over on the slippery dance floor, in front of millions of people watching on TV.

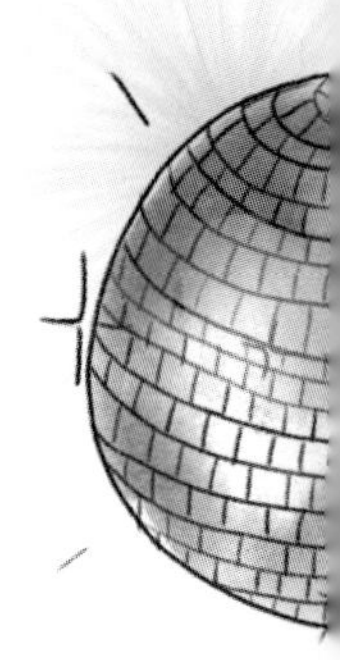

Chapter Eight

Simon Shimmer helped Mabel up. "Not to worry," he whispered. "Happens to the best of us!" He smiled, and took her hand. "Now, let's dance!"

But something had changed in Mabel's feet. Just as suddenly as they had started dancing, they stopped dancing.

Mabel tried to do the moves she'd been able to do minutes before – and found her dancing feet had deserted her.

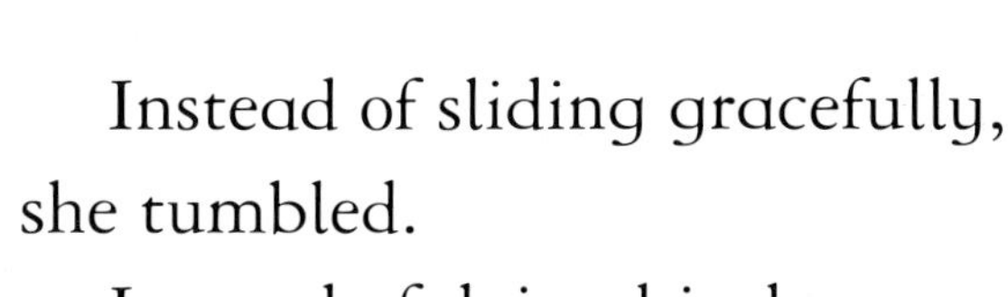

Instead of sliding gracefully, she tumbled.

Instead of doing hip-hop moves, she stumbled.

Instead of tapping and twisting, she staggered and slipped.

Simon Shimmer did his best to help. He took Mabel's hands and danced her in and out of the glittery goal, but it was clearly not the grand finale with the Girl with Dancing Feet which everyone had been hoping for. Mabel could hear the audience whispering and getting restless in their seats.

As Simon Shimmer whirled her around the dance floor, she caught sight of her mum and dad's faces, looking worried. Dora mouthed at her, "What's going on?"

"I don't know!" Mabel mouthed back. She was close to tears as Simon Shimmer twirled her around for one last time and she lost her balance yet again. Her clumsiness had returned, just at the wrong moment.

This was a disaster – a dancing disaster.

And then, just as it felt as if things couldn't possibly get any worse, they suddenly did.

"Look out!" yelled a stagehand.

The glitter ball above them had begun to spin faster and faster.

"Look out!" shouted Mabel's mum.

The glitter ball whirled so fast it was now a golden blur.

"Look out!" yelled Ted Turner. "It's going to fall!"

The glitter ball spun off the screw which held it on to the ceiling, twisting crazily ...

and flew into the air.

Simon Shimmer stopped, mid-dance. The orchestra tootled into silence. Everyone watched, in horror, as the glitter ball whooshed down from the ceiling.

"It's going to hit you, Mabel!" shouted Dora.

"No – it's going to hit Simon!" yelled Ted Turner.

Simon Shimmer suddenly seemed to have been frozen to the spot.

"What do I do?" he whispered. "What's the dance move for this? This has never happened before!" He quivered in the spotlight as the giant glitter ball hurtled towards him.

Mabel Green, however, felt her footballing instincts come flooding back. What was it her dad had said? "Trust your feet."

And so, as the glitter ball flew towards Simon Shimmer, Mabel caught it with one foot, flicked it on to the other …

… and shot it safely away, straight into the glittery goal.

Chapter Nine

There was complete silence for a moment – and then the whole studio erupted into wild cheers. Mabel Green was almost flattened by the audience as they pelted on to the dance floor to congratulate her.

"Go, Mabel!" cheered Dora.

"Yeah, right, well done, what skills!" said Ted Turner.

Mabel's mum and dad didn't say anything. They just looked very, very proud.

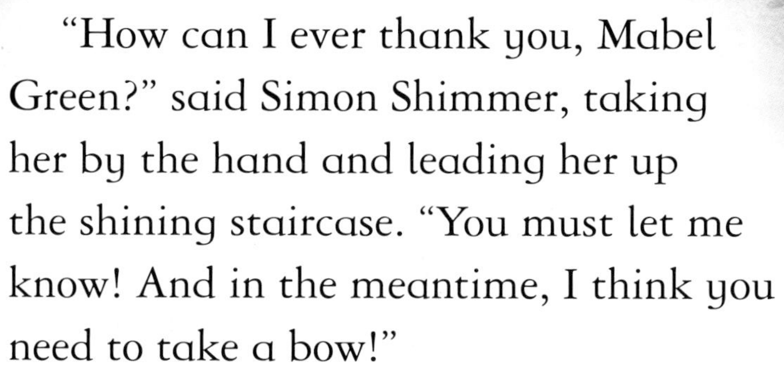

"How can I ever thank you, Mabel Green?" said Simon Shimmer, taking her by the hand and leading her up the shining staircase. "You must let me know! And in the meantime, I think you need to take a bow!"

Mabel couldn't believe her eyes as she looked down at the crowd of people below her, clapping and cheering.

She took a breath, smiled, bowed – and did not fall over.

It turned out that Mabel Green was not a footballer nor a dancer – but a little bit of both.

The following Saturday morning, the Jesmond Juniors football pitch was deserted. The goals hung empty. The grass was green and smooth.

The usual Saturday morning practice session had been cancelled, so that the team could attend their first specialist training session.

Their coach had booked these special sessions after Mabel Green's twinkle-toed triumph against Thugsford, and then her spectacular goal on *Come Dance with Me*. They had been paid for by Simon Shimmer himself.

Yes, on the other side of town, the Jesmond Juniors football team was doing ballet lessons.

Mabel Green and her team *loved* ballet lessons.

After reading activities

Quick quiz

See how fast you can answer these questions! Look back at the story if you can't remember.

What is Mabel's football team called?

What happens to Mabel's feet when she's talking to Simon Shimmer on the phone?

Why does the TV studio audience congratulate Mabel?

Talk about it!

How would you feel if you suddenly got the chance to appear on a TV show? Which show would you most like to appear on? What might happen?

1) Jesmond Juniors; 2) they start tap-dancing; 3) she stopped the glitter ball from falling on Simon Shimmer